Crocodiles

A Level One Reader

By Cynthia Klingel and Robert B. Noyed

The Child's World®

What has a long nose
and a very long tail?
A crocodile!

Crocodiles live in water.

Crocodiles live where it is warm.

Crocodiles have long bodies and short legs.

Crocodiles are dark brown and green.

Their skin is very thick
and bumpy.

Crocodiles have many sharp teeth.

They hide in the water
to hunt for food.

Crocodiles have very strong jaws.

Crocodiles can be scary!

Word List

bodies

bumpy

hunt

jaws

tail

thick

Note to Parents and Educators

Welcome to The Wonders of Reading™! These books provide text at three different levels for beginning readers to practice and strengthen their reading skills. In addition, the use of nonfiction text gives readers the valuable opportunity to *read to learn*, not just to learn to read.

These leveled readers allow children to choose books at their level of reading confidence and performance. Level One books offer beginning readers simple language, word choice, and sentence structure as well as a word list. Level Two books feature slightly more difficult vocabulary, longer sentences, and longer total text. In the back of each Level Two book are an index and a list of books and Web sites for finding out more information. Level Three books continue to extend word choice and length of text. In the back of each Level Three book are a glossary, an index, and a list of books and Web sites for further research.

State and national standards in reading and language arts emphasize using nonfiction at all levels of reading development. The Wonders of Reading™ books fill the historical void in nonfiction for primary grade readers with the additional benefit of a leveled text.

About the Authors

Cynthia Klingel has worked as a high school English teacher and an elementary teacher. She is currently the curriculum director for a Minnesota school district. Writing children's books is another way for her to continue her passion for sharing the written word with children. Cynthia is a frequent visitor to the children's section of bookstores and enjoys spending time with her many friends, family, and two daughters.

Robert Noyed started his career as a newspaper reporter. Since then, he has worked in communications and public relations for more than fourteen years for a Minnesota school district. He enjoys writing books for children and finds that it brings a different feeling of challenge and accomplishment from other writing projects. He is an avid reader who also enjoys music, theater, traveling, and spending time with his wife, son, and daughter.

Published by The Child's World®, Inc.

PO Box 326
Chanhassen, MN 55317-0326
800-599-READ
www.childsworld.com

Photo Credits
© 2000 E. R. Degginger/Dembinsky Photo Assoc. Inc.: 5
© 1993 Fritz Polking/Dembinsky Photo Assoc. Inc.: 13
© 1999 Fritz Polking/Dembinsky Photo Assoc. Inc.: 14
© James P. Rowan: 6, 9
© Joe McDonald/Tom Stack & Associates: 18, 21
© 1995 Mark J. Thomas/Dembinsky Photo Assoc. Inc.: cover
© Martin Withers FRPS/Dembinsky Photo Assoc. Inc.: 17
© Robert E. Barber/Unicorn Stock Photos: 10
© W. Perry Conway/Tom Stack & Associates: 2

Project Coordination: Editorial Directions, Inc.
Photo Research: Alice K. Flanagan

Library of Congress Cataloging-in-Publication Data
Klingel, Cynthia Fitterer.
Crocodiles / by Cynthia Klingel and Robert B. Noyed.
    p. cm.
ISBN 1-56766-942-5 (lib. bdg. : alk. paper)
1. Crocodiles—Juvenile literature. [1. Crocodiles.] I. Noyed, Robert B. II. Title.
QL666.C925 K65 2001
597.98'2—dc21
                        00-011360